# THE GOLDEN GOOSE

## Barbara Reid

Adapted from the traditional fairy tale by the Brothers Grimm

**North Winds Press**

A Division of Scholastic Canada Ltd.

This book was designed in QuarkXPress,
with type set in 16 point Giovanni Book.

The illustrations for this book were made with Plasticine
that is shaped and pressed onto illustration board.
Acrylic paint and other materials are used for special effects.

Photography by Ian Crysler.

**Scholastic Canada Ltd.**
175 Hillmount Road, Markham, Ontario, Canada L6C 1Z7

**Scholastic Inc.**
555 Broadway, New York, NY 10012, USA

**Scholastic Australia Pty Limited**
PO Box 579, Gosford, NSW 2250, Australia

**Scholastic New Zealand Limited**
Private Bag 94407, Greenmount, Auckland, New Zealand

**Scholastic Ltd.**
Villiers House, Clarendon Avenue, Leamington Spa,
Warwickshire CV32 5PR, UK

**Canadian Cataloguing in Publication Data**

Reid, Barbara, 1957-
The golden goose

ISBN 0-439-98719-9

I. Title.

PS8585.E4484G64 2000          jC813'.54          C00-930819-9
PZ8.R262Go 2000

5 4 3 2 1          Printed and bound in Canada          0 1 2 3 4 /0

For Ian.

Once upon a time, in a northern town, there lived a wealthy merchant by the name of Leroy King. Of all his possessions, he most treasured his only child.

One morning he woke his daughter early. "No peeking . . ." he whispered as he led her outside. "Surprise!"

The girl opened her eyes and gasped. Her favourite climbing tree had been cut down. The brambles that had sheltered so many birds had been cleared away. The frog pond had been paved over.

"Happy Birthday, Princess!" her father boomed.

"My name is Gwendolyn," she wailed, fleeing to her room.

Leroy sighed. "Sixteen years without a smile! I've spent a fortune and nothing makes my Princess happy. What can I do?"

Deep in the forest above the town lived a woodcutter's widow and her three sons. The widow was as proud of her two older sons as they were of themselves. No one thought much of the youngest, Rupert, a daydreamer.

"Oh, Drupert, is your head as full of acorns as your pockets? I asked you to fetch my moustache brush!" the oldest would say.

"Stop talking to your little bird friends, Droopy, and get me a fresh toothpick," the second son would order.

Even their mother joined in: "Quit mucking about the swamp and clean your brothers' boots!"

Rupert took it all with good humour.

One morning the widow called for her eldest son.

"It is time for you to take up your father's axe. Go into the forest and cut us some wood. You are so handsome and clever, I know you will make us our fortune." She packed his knapsack with a Chelsea bun and a jug of cider to refresh him as he worked.

He had not gone far into the woods when he met an old, grey man.

"Oh, I am so hungry," the old man cried. "Oh, I am so thirsty! Would you have a morsel or a drop to share with me, sir?"

"Share with *you*?" the young man scoffed. "If I give a portion to you, there will be that much less for me. Begone!"

Pleased with his cleverness, he picked out a fine tree. But with his first swing he cut his arm and had to run home to his mother.

The next day the widow packed a tin of butter tarts and a jug of lemonade and sent her second son into the forest. "You are so big and strong," she said, "I know you will succeed!"

Not very far along he, too, met the old, grey man.

"Oh, I am weak with hunger and thirst!" said the old man. "Please sir, would you spare me some of your food and drink?"

"Ho ho!" laughed the second son. "I didn't get to be this big and strong by giving away my food! Out of my way."

With that, he stepped up to a tree and took a mighty swing with the axe. But it slipped and cut his leg so badly he limped all the way home.

On the third day Rupert said, "Today I will go into the forest."

"Nonsense!" his mother said. "Your brothers both came to harm, and you are not nearly as handsome, clever, big or strong as they are."

But Rupert begged until his mother agreed. There was nothing left for him to take but a crust of dry bread and a jar of well water.

Soon Rupert came across the old man.

"Oh, I am dying of hunger and thirst!" he groaned. "Would you have a crumb or a sip to spare?"

"I have only bread and water, but I would be happy to share," Rupert offered.

But when he reached into his pocket, Rupert was surprised to find a silver flask of hot chocolate and a sack of doughnuts. He and the old man ate and drank their fill.

"Your kindness shall be rewarded," the old man said. "Search this tree and you will find good fortune."

He gave a bow and was gone.

Rupert looked the tree up and down. Then he walked around it. There, nestled in a hole, was a goose. But this was no ordinary goose, for every one of its feathers was pure gold.

"What a rare and beautiful creature! I must share this discovery. Come along, Goldie." Rupert tucked the goose under his arm and set out for town.

By sunset he had reached the edge of the forest. There was a roadside inn, and Rupert decided to spend the night. For the price of his silver flask, one of the innkeeper's daughters showed him to a room, never taking her eyes off the golden goose.

"Just one of those feathers would make me rich!" she thought.

When all was quiet that night, the girl crept into Rupert's room. Taking hold of the goose, she tried to pluck a feather, only to find that her hand was stuck tight.

"Help!" she cried. "Marie!"

Her sister came running.
"Therese! What have you got there, eh? Let me see!"
She took her sister by the waist to pull her away, but found that she, too, was stuck. That was how they spent the night.

Rupert woke at sunrise. "Good morning, Goldie!" he said. And with the goose tucked under his arm he set off, heedless of the two girls trailing behind.

A coachman waiting for his breakfast spied the sisters running after Rupert.

"Therese! Marie! My omelette!"

But when he caught hold of Marie's apron string, the coachman was caught himself.

As they passed the schoolhouse, the schoolmistress called out to the coachman, "You're going to be late!"

She snatched at his sleeve, but she stuck like glue and had to fall in line.

16

As Rupert and his troop rounded the corner into town, Elvira Nettle leaped out from behind a bush.

"Out of my tulips, you hooligans!" She reached to tweak the schoolmistress's ear and before she knew it she was tottering down King Street behind the others.

"Help!" she squeaked as they came alongside Farmer Plotz. He reached for the old woman's arm, and away he went too, stuck tight.

The barber saw his next customer disappearing and gave chase. Soon he was joined to the end of the rag-tag parade as it made its way toward the edge of Leroy King's estate.

That morning, Leroy was as gloomy as his daughter. He had offered half his wealth to anyone who could make her happy. Alas, when Gwendolyn stepped out of the front door and saw the crowd of fortune-seekers, her frown only deepened.

"Father!" She stamped her foot. "My mood is not to be bargained with. Call off this contest at once!"

"Sorry, boys," a defeated Leroy announced.

At that moment Goldie, Rupert, Therese, Marie, the coachman, the schoolmistress, Elvira Nettle, Farmer Plotz and the barber came staggering into the courtyard like a crazy train.

Three things happened at once: Gwendolyn broke into an irresistible peal of merry laughter. The spell was broken, freeing the prisoners. And Rupert's heart was captured.

Gwendolyn came forward and held out her hand. "I'm Gwendolyn."

Dazzled by her smile, Rupert blushed. "I'm Rupert, and this is Goldie."

Gwendolyn gave a delighted laugh and whispered to her father. "Daddy, I believe you have an offer to make this charming young man?"

Leroy could hardly believe his ears and eyes. Still, he kept his wits about him.

"Well done, young fellow. I'm pleased to see you've brought some happiness to my Princess. But can you guarantee it will last? Here's my proposal. If you can get my little girl to smile three more times, we have a deal!"

Rupert gazed at Gwendolyn, enchanted. "I collect acorns," he told her. He pulled a handful from his pocket and offered her one. "If you care for this, it will grow into a magnificent tree."

"How lovely!" Gwendolyn's cheeks dimpled.

From the edge of the forest a bird twittered. Rupert gave an answering whistle and, quick as a wink, a chickadee landed on his shoulder. Gwendolyn's eyes sparkled.

Rupert kept whistling until the courtyard filled with birds. Gwendolyn beamed.

"Honk!" The golden goose pecked excitedly at the ground. "Honk! Honk!"

Rupert put his ear to the ground and listened, then pulled up a paving stone. Water burbled up through the hole.

"There's a spring under here." Rupert pointed. "It would make a nice spot for a pond."

Gwendolyn threw her arms around Rupert's neck with a squeal of joy. Leroy pumped Rupert's hand. "Congratulations, son!"

The crowd cheered, and Leroy invited the whole town to a party. "Spare no expense!" he cried. They all feasted and danced and made merry for days.

And Rupert and Gwendolyn were so happy in each other's company that they are together to this very day.